The Boy and the Quilt

by **Shirley Kurtz**
Illustrated by Cheryl Benner

Good Books®
Intercourse, PA 17534
Printed in Mexico
C.I.P. data may be found on page 32

The boy's sister was going to make a quilt, and so was his mother. And so, she said, could he.

He thought making a quilt might be easy, or at least fun, and it would be, sometimes. Other times, though, it would seem like a chore, like feeding the dog or mowing the lawn.

Only the dog was always hungry and the grass kept right on growing. But when the boy would be finished with his patches, his mother would quilt them. Then the quilt would be done forever, and it would be his and he could sleep under it.

The boy's mother collected scraps of cloth from his grandma and aunts and cousins. And she made three piles—the red and green pieces were for her quilt, the yellows and browns were for his sister's, and other brown pieces and all the blues were for the boy.

He kept his scraps all junked together in a bag somewhere.

One morning during breakfast his mother cut two holes out of the cereal box. It was time he got started on his patches, she said, and he would need some cardboard.
Cardboard patches?
And there was still cereal in the box!

Now where were his scraps?

The boy dug through his bag and pulled out some blue and white stripes, brown checks, brown and blue plaid. The cloth was all smashed and wrinkled from being jammed in the bag. So his mother set up the ironing board. (It would stay up so long as nobody leaned against it.)

He put his cardboard atop the warm blue and white cloth on the ironing board, just so, and drew the whole way around it with a pen. Then he drew more squares, all up against each other like windowpanes.

Cutting along the ink lines made patches—well, maybe. Sometimes the cloth slipped and slid between the boy's scissors. Rats. That patch wasn't square anymore. His mother said he'd have to throw it away, but the next one looked pretty good.

Two piles of squares, big squares and little squares (the ones that hadn't gotten their sides chopped off), slowly grew higher and higher. Sometimes the boy wished he could stop.

Slowly more patches, and more. He kept them all upstairs in his underwear drawer. But there was hardly enough space.

His sister's patches were in an old shoe box underneath her bed and already she had stitched some together on the sewing machine. The boy liked the sewing machine. There were threads going through holes, and wheels that spun and a needle that jumped when you ran the motor.

Upstairs, the boy took four little patches off the piles beside his underwear. A blue patch, a dark brown, a brown-and-white checked, a brown-and-white striped. He would sew them together into a square.

"Shouldn't there be more blue?" his mother wondered. "Or wouldn't it look better with the dark brown between the checks and stripes?"

"It's my quilt," said the boy.

"You're right, it is," said his mother.

The boy held the patches together while the machine hummed and hopped.

Rats. The stripes were wrong side up. "Here," said his mother. "I'll rip out those stitches for you."

More jumping and hopping and humming and now the boy had a square. It was just a little crooked. This patched piece and another one, plus two patches off the stack of big ones in his drawer, all stitched together, would make a block. More and more blocks would make a quilt, and there would be room again for his underwear.

"We'll sew plain blue cloth between the blocks and all around the edges," said his mother.

"Oh no," said the boy. "I want the patches all clumped together. Nothing between them."

"But that will look crazy," said his mother. Her own quilt was on her bed by now, all proper and quite beautiful.

"I like it this way. It's my quilt," said the boy.

"It won't look right," said his mother. "But it is your quilt."

And when all his patches were sewn together into one big, wonderful, crazy piece, the boy's job was done.

Around the edges his mother sewed some of the blue cloth she bought at the store, and she drew lines, and along one side she put his name all straight and proud.

And then one morning the boy and his mother hauled the kitchen table into the living room, and the mother swept and washed the kitchen floor. She laid more blue cloth on the floor, and stuffing over it, and the boy's patchwork on the very top. She sat on the floor all day and pinned and sewed everything together.

She said it made her back hurt. But it was fun eating lunch in the living room.

Now his patchwork went into the hoop by the big window, and while she stitched lines and X's and diamonds, the boy's mother told stories and listened to country music on WFRB. Sometimes the boy read to her and then they were each doing the other a favor.

Nobody was supposed to play under the hoop.

But one night when they were all playing hide-and-seek inside, in the dark, the boy's father could not find the mother for a very long time.

Other people, the mother said, wore thimbles when they quilted, but not her. She said sewing with a thimble was like walking around with a bucket over your head. But sometimes she put a Band-Aid on her thumb to keep it from getting sore from the needle poking up and down through all the layers of the quilt.

The sister claimed she was going to quilt her own patchwork, but the boy didn't quite believe this. Their mother just said, "Hmmm," and "We'll see."

Finally one day the boy's mother pulled more cloth out of his scrap bag, for making the edges.

And before long, his quilt was finished.

It had stopped growing; it would never be hungry and it would never need to be mowed. It would always be his, and on cold nights he would be warm.

Directions for Making a Quilt Like the Boy's

For patterns, cut 4¼″ and 8″ squares from graph paper, trace them on cardboard, and cut out. The large patches will be equal in size to four small patches sewn together. All seams should be ¼″.

When marking patches, place patterns in line with the grain of the fabrics and use indelible ink. You will need to cut 120 small patches and 30 large ones for a single-bed size quilt, or 160 small and 40 large ones for a double-bed size. Use only soft cottons and cotton blends. Old, not-too-worn clothing can be cut up for a "memory" quilt.

To assemble a block, lay two small patches with right sides together, pin, and stitch along one edge, allowing a ¼″ seam allowance. Repeat with another pair of small patches. Then lay the pairs right side together, pin, and stitch along one side. Next pin and stitch this four-patch square to an 8″ square, making a half-block. Piece another half-block and stitch the halves together.

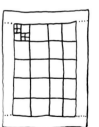

Half-block

Make 15 blocks for twin-bed size, 20 blocks for double-bed size.

Seam edges can face in either direction (if possible, toward darker fabrics) but they should not lie open.

To put together the quilt top, arrange the completed blocks, pin and sew them in strips, then sew the strips together. Press the patchwork. Cut your border fabric into desired widths and sew them to the patchwork. (Quilting will reduce the size about two inches.)

Use a #2 pencil **to mark quilting lines.** (They will eventually rub off or wash out.) Your quilting should be no closer than ¼″ to the seams. Lines along any seams need not be marked, but the X's and diamonds must be drawn to meet those lines.

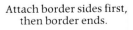

Attach border sides first, then border ends.

Draw X's on the big squares.   Put diamonds on the borders.

For the name on your quilt, draw and cut paper letters. Pin these patterns atop assorted scraps like those used in your patchwork. The scraps should be reinforced with lightweight iron-on interfacing. Cut fabric letters, allowing extra for seams. Pin the letters (with seam edges slashed and folded under) onto the border of the quilt top and machine-stitch.

You may need to piece your **backing fabric.** It should extend several inches beyond the quilt top on all sides, and the backing seams should be pressed open. **Batting** can be purchased in various sizes; if you must piece it, use long stitches. The batting should also be several inches longer and wider than the quilt top.

Pieced batting

Working on the floor with the backing right-side-down, patchwork right-side-up, and batting in between, pin through all layers with extra-long straight pins about eight inches apart. Then baste with long running stitches in lines about four inches apart.

To quilt, use a hoop at least 14″ in diameter. (A hoop on a stand is inexpensive and takes up less space than the traditional quilting frame, and with any hoop the patchwork can be turned in any direction for greater ease in quilting.) Quilting thread is extra sturdy and a quilting needle is tiny.

Use a long, single strand of thread and **begin quilting** with a hidden single knot. As you quilt, take several stitches onto your needle before pulling the thread through. (Be sure the needle is piercing all layers.) End your seam with a backstitch.

Cut scraps on the bias.

After quilting is completed, trim away the excess backing and batting. For the edging, cut scraps 3″ wide and varying lengths, with ends cut at an angle. Piece these scraps together until you have four strips, one for each side of the quilt and measuring several inches longer than each side. Fold each strip in half, right-side-out, and pin and stitch the strip edges to the topside edge of the quilt through all layers. Then fold the strip over the quilt edge, pin, and hem.

Finally, remove basting threads.

Pin and machine-stitch the folded edging to the quilt top through all layers.

Directions for Making a Comforter

Your patchwork can be made into a knotted comforter instead of a quilt. Knotting is speedier and easier than quilting, and no hoop is needed.

Assemble your patches and border fabric as for a quilt. Baste together the top, batting and backing.

Spread the basted comforter flat over a large tabletop to work. You will need to make knots at the corners and center of every large square and every four-patch square, and throughout the border at equal intervals.

Thread a 2½″ darning needle with a long double strand of sturdy crocheting thread (enough for several knots). For each knot, make a small single stitch with 3″ tails. Be sure the full stitch shows on the underside of the comforter. Tie the tails in a square knot and pull tight without puckering the patchwork.

Trim and edge your comforter as for a quilt. Remove basting threads.

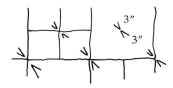

Pull knot tight.

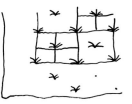

Measure for border knots and mark with #2 pencil.

All stitches (except ones in centers of large squares and in border) cross patchwork seams.

About the Author

Shirley Kurtz lives near Keyser, West Virginia, with her husband, Paulson, and children.

They started on their quilts when Christopher was seven and Jennifer ten. Several years later, now, Zachary is working on his.

The scraps came from the Miller cousins (Ann and her girls, and Grace) and Aunt Valerie and Grandma Baer.

About the Artist

Cheryl Benner is an artist and designer who lives near Lancaster, Pennsylvania with her husband and young son. She is co-author and designer with Rachel Thomas Pellman of *The Country Love Quilt, The Country Lily Quilt, The Country Songbird Quilt, The Country Bride Quilt Collection* and *The Country Paradise Quilt.*

Cover illustration and design by Cheryl Benner

The Boy and the Quilt
Copyright © 1991 by Good Books, Intercourse, PA 17534
International Standard Book Number: 1-56148-009-6
Library of Congress Catalog Card Number: 91-74050

Printed in Mexico.

Library of Congress Cataloging-in-Publication Data
Kurtz, Shirley.
    The boy and the quilt / Shirley Kurtz;
illustrations by Cheryl A. Benner.
        p. cm.
    Summary: With a little help from his mother and sister, a young boy makes a quilt of his own.
    ISBN 1-56148-009-6: $6.95
    (1. Quilting—Fiction. 2. Family life—Fiction.) I. Benner, Cheryl A., 1962- ill. II. Title.
PZ7.K9628Bo 1991
(E)—dc20   91-74050
                                                      CIP
                                                      AC